Plane's
Royal Rescue

Peter Bently

Illustrated by Bella Bee and Lucy Fleming

NEW BURLINGTON

Plane is at the airport preparing for a **flight**.

Captain Koala and his co-pilot watch as a **fuel truck** fills up the fuel tanks.

Luggage is loaded from a luggage cart into the **hold**.

A **pushback tug** is attached to Plane's **front wheels**.

A black limousine drives up
to a private jet nearby.

"It's the king and his family,"
says Captain Koala to his co-pilot.
"They're flying to the same airport as us."

A **bus** brings the **passengers** to Plane.

While they are **boarding**, the pilots
check everything in the **cockpit**.

There are lots of **dials** and
switches and computer screens.

The **royal jet** is now leaving. The limousine driver waves frantically at the **king's pilot**. But the pilot does not see him.

Captain Koala goes to **find out** what the matter is.

"The king's forgotten his **crown!**"
says the driver.

"**Don't worry,**" smiles
Captain Koala. "I have an idea."

Plane's doors **close**. The boarding stairs
are rolled away. It's time to go!

Captain Koala starts the **huge jets.**
They **whirr** into life. The pilots check their
computers to make sure everything is working.

The **tug** pushes Plane back from the **terminal**. Then the tug drives clear.

The co-pilot **powers** up the engines.

Plane moves towards the **runway**.

Captain Koala speaks on the **intercom**.
He wishes the passengers a **good flight**.

Plane
waits near
the runway.

A huge cargo jet takes off.

"You are clear for take off!"
says the air traffic controller.

Plane moves to the
start of the **runway**.

WHOOSH!

Captain Koala puts the
engines on **full power**.

Plane **speeds** down the runway and **takes off.**

ROAR!

THUNK!

Plane **tucks** in its wheels.

Plane **climbs** above the **clouds**
and into the sunshine.

The flight is **very smooth**.
Plane flies over **mountains** and **seas**.

At last Plane **descends** towards its destination. The wheels **come down**.

CLUNK!

As they land Captain Koala puts the engines into **reverse** to slow down.

ROAR!

Plane **taxies** to the terminal.

The **boarding steps** are moved into place.
Buses are waiting for the passengers.

As they leave, their luggage is
unloaded onto a **luggage cart**.

The royal jet is already
at the **terminal**.

"But **where** is my crown?"
asks a very **worried** king.
"I have an **important** event today!"

"Your Majesty, here is your crown,"
says Captain Koala. "We looked after
it **very** carefully in the cockpit!"

"Thank you, Captain Koala!" says the king.

"And thanks to **Plane!**" says Captain Koala.

Let's look at
Plane

Wing flaps

Passenger door

Cockpit

Hold

Jet engine

Tail

Passenger door

Hold

Wing

Other Airport Vehicles

Turboprop airliner

Pushback tug

Luggage cart

Helicopter

A NEW BURLINGTON BOOK

Designer: Rachel Lawston
Art Director: Laura Roberts-Jensen
Editors: Tasha Percy and Sophie Hallam
Editorial Director: Victoria Garrard

First published in hardback in the UK in 2015 by
QED Publishing
Part of The Quarto Group
The Old Brewery, 6 Blundell Street
London, N7 9BH

MIX
Paper from
responsible sources
FSC® C016973
FSC
www.fsc.org

A catalogue record for this book is available from the British Library.

ISBN: 978 1 78493 798 0

Printed in China